First published in Great Britain 2005 by Walker Books Ltd
87 Vauxhall Walk, London SE11 5HJ

20 19 18 17 16

©2004 Mo Willems

First published in the United States by Hyperion Books for Children.
British publication rights arranged with Sheldon Fogelman Agency, Inc.

The right of Mo Willems to be identified as author and illustrator of this work has
been asserted by him in accordance with the Copyright, Designs and Patents Act 1988

The images in this book are a melding of hand-drawn ink sketches and digital photography
in a computer (where the sketches were coloured and shaded, the photographs given their
sepia tone and sundry air conditioners, garbage cans and industrial debris expunged).

This book has been typeset in Coop Light and Village-Roman

Printed in China. All rights reserved.

British Library Cataloguing in Publication Data:
a catalogue record for this book is available from the British Library

ISBN 978-1-84428-059-9

www.walkerbooks.co.uk

WALKER BOOKS
AND SUBSIDIARIES

LONDON · BOSTON · SYDNEY · AUCKLAND

KNUFFLE BUNNY

A CAUTIONARY TALE BY Mo Willems

Not very long ago, before
she could even speak words,
Trixie went on an errand
with her daddy...

Trixie and her daddy went down the street,

and into the Laundromat.

Trixie helped her daddy put the washing into the machine.

She was even allowed to put the money into the machine.

Then they left.

But on the
way home ...

Trixie **realized**

something.

Trixie turned to her daddy and said,

"Now, please don't get fussy," said her daddy.

Well, she had no choice...

Trixie bawled.

She went boneless.

She did everything she could to show how unhappy she was.

By the time they got home, her daddy was unhappy, too.

As soon as Trixie's mummy opened the door, she asked,

The whole family ran down the street.

And they ran through the park.

They zoomed past the school

and into the Laundromat.

Trixie's daddy looked for Knuffle Bunny.

And looked ...

and looked ...

and looked...

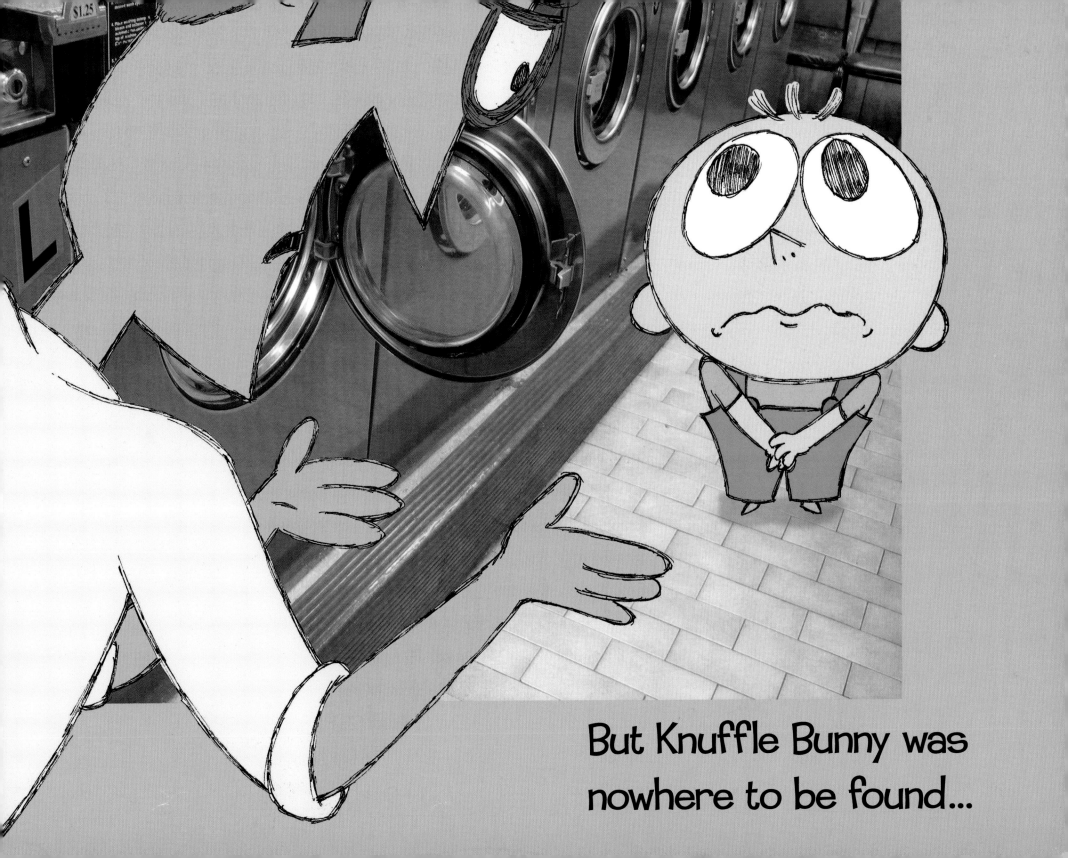

But Knuffle Bunny was
nowhere to be found...

So Trixie's daddy
decided to look harder.

Until ...

And those were the first words Trixie ever said.

This book is dedicated to
the real Trixie and her mummy.
Special thanks to
Anne and Alessandra;
Noah, Megan and Edward;
the 358 6th Avenue Laundromat;
and my neighbours in Park Slope, Brooklyn.